SOPHIE the ZILLIONAIRE

Finding the right name isn't easy!
See what else Sophie tries out....

1: SOPHIE the AWESOME

2: SOPHIE the HERO

3: SOPHIE the CHATTERBOX

4: SOPHIE the ZILLIONAIRE

5: SOPHIE the SNOOP

6: SOPHIE the DAREDEVIL

SOPHIE the ZILLIONAIRE

by Lara Bergen

illustrated by Laura Tallardy

SCHOLASTIC INC.

New York Toronto London Auckland

Sydney Mexico City New Delhi Hong Kong

To Syd, for a zillion reasons

ISBN 978-0-545-14607-4

12 11 10 9 8 7 6 5 4 3 2 1 11 12 13 14 15 16/0

Printed in the U.S.A. 40
First printing, January 2011
Designed by Tim Hall

CHAPTER 1

Sophie stared at the thing in her hand. She turned it over carefully. It was paper, and it was green, and it had the number fifty all over it.

That was because it was fifty whole dollars!

Sophie could not believe it.

"I can't believe it!" she said to Kate Barry, who was standing beside her. Kate was Sophie's very best friend. "It's fifty whole dollars!"

Sophie looked down at the grass next to the sidewalk. That was where she had picked up the fifty-dollar bill. She hoped that there was even more money there! But there was not.

Still. She had fifty whole dollars. She was probably the richest girl in the whole world, she guessed.

(Well . . . maybe she wasn't richer than a princess. But she was richer than any ordinary girl in Ordinary, Virginia, she bet!)

Sophie wanted so badly to be special. Now she really was! And to think all she had to do was look down as she walked home from the bus stop.

"Where do you think it came from?" Kate asked her as they started to walk.

Sophie shrugged. "I don't know."

Then she got a feeling. It was not good. For Sophie to find money, someone else must have lost it first. But there was no one else around.

Sophie started to feel better. There wasn't anybody to ask. Plus didn't her big sister, Hayley, always say, "Finders keepers, losers sweepers"?

Sophie wasn't sure why losers had to sweep. But that was their problem. The fifty dollars was hers!

"So what are you going to do with it?" Kate asked. She grinned and licked her lips. "I think you should buy lots of gum!"

Sophie knew that Kate liked gum. A lot. This was mostly because her mom did not buy it—not since Kate chewed some, then tried to keep it behind her ear. It worked for a girl in a movie they saw. But it did not work for Kate. It got stuck in her hair, and her mom had to cut it out. Kate looked funny for a while. But she still liked gum just as much after all that.

Sophie thought about gum for a minute, then shook her head. "I'm going to keep the money. And tomorrow at school I'm going to tell everyone about it!" she said.

Sophie could picture the kids in her class. They would be amazed that she was so rich. They would never again call her just plain Sophie . . . or Sophie M. . . . or even Sophie Miller.

Sophie waved the bill. "Thanks to this, I will be Sophie the Rich. No, wait!" She thought of something even better. "I will be Sophie the

Zillionaire!" Sophie gave the fifty dollars a big kiss. "What do you think?" she asked Kate.

Kate shrugged. "I'd still buy gum. But it *is* a better name than Sophie the Honest," she said, grinning.

Sophie smiled back. Kate was the best. Sophie was very, very, very glad that they were friends again. Luckily, Kate had forgiven her for spilling a secret. Sophie had just been trying to be Sophie the Honest. That was the special name she had tried out before. Who knew it would cause so much trouble?

Sophie would not make that mistake again. One thing was for sure: Secrets would be safe with Sophie the Zillionaire!

Then suddenly, a thought popped into Sophie's head. This fifty dollars wasn't all the money she had. She had a bank full of money in her room.

Sophie grabbed Kate's arm. "Come on!" she said. "Let's go to my house and see how much there is in my bank to add to this!"

Kate shifted her backpack to the other

shoulder. "Sounds good!" she said. Then she stopped. "Ohhh, I can't."

"Why?" Sophie asked. Kate wasn't still mad at her, was she?

Kate made a blah face. "I have to get home for my piano lesson."

"Aw." Sophie nodded. She was disappointed. (But very relieved that Kate wasn't mad, too!)

She wondered if you could pay a piano teacher *not* to teach. Did she have enough money for that? Hmm...

☆ ☆ ☆

"Mom, I'm home! And I'm rich!" Sophie yelled as she burst through the kitchen door.

Her mom stopped pouring iced tea. She held a finger to her lips. "Sophie, please—keep it down!" She nodded at the ceiling. "Max is napping upstairs," she whispered.

Sophie frowned. She did not understand. "Is he sick?"

Max was her brother. He was two. And he *never* took naps.

Her mom shook her head. "No. But he yawned, so I thought I'd try," she said. Then she took a sip of tea and smiled. "So, what do you mean by 'I'm rich'?"

Sophie held up her new fifty-dollar bill with both hands. "I mean this! It's fifty dollars!"

She thought her mom's smile would get bigger. But instead, it started to shrink. Her mom's eyes sure got bigger, though. "Where did that come from?"

"The sidewalk," Sophie said.

"You mean you found it?" her mom asked.

Sophie nodded proudly. "Yep!"

Sophie's mom didn't look any happier. "Well, someone must have dropped it. Did you ask everyone on the street?" she asked.

Sophie shrugged. "I wanted to. But there wasn't anyone to ask," she said.

BAM!

THUD!

THUMP-THUMP-THUMP-THUMP-THUMP-THUMP...

Sophie looked up. She knew those sounds well. They were the sounds of Max jumping out of his crib and knocking things down.

Her mom looked up, too, and sighed. She turned back to Sophie.

"That's a lot of money to find, Sophie," she said. "But it's a lot to lose, also. I think you should ask all our neighbors if they lost fifty dollars. If they say yes, you'll have done a good thing by returning it. If they say no, you can keep the money."

THUMP-THUMP-THUMP-THUMP . . .

CRASH!

Sophie's mom put down her glass and stood up. "Here I come, Maxie!" she yelled.

☆ ☆ ☆

A little while later, Sophie left the house with heavy shoulders. But she came back with a big smile.

She had asked all the people on her street if they had lost money. And they had all said no!

Plus she had gotten lots of "What a *good* girl you are to ask's"!

It almost made her think her name should be Sophie the Good. But "Good" was so boring compared to "Zillionaire." No. She would stick with the name she had picked. Especially now that she was allowed to keep the fifty dollars.

At last, it was time for Sophie the Zillionaire to see how much money she had!

Sophie ran up to her room. She shared it with her sister, Hayley, who was ten. It had been *all* Hayley's room until Sophie was born. And Hayley always reminded her of that.

Sophie went to the bookcase that was all hers. She grabbed her horse bank off the shelf.

Sophie's horse bank was one of her favorite things. She had painted it at her friend Eve's birthday at the pottery-painting place. That was the day she decided that horses were her favorite animal. After dolphins. And kittens. And meerkats.

The horse's legs were folded, like it was lying on the ground. It was mostly brown, like a real horse, but it had a long rainbow tail. It made Sophie very proud.

The horse bank was much better than the coffee mug she had painted another time. That had been for her dad. She had tried to paint a picture of him on it, but he thought it was Tiptoe, their kitten. She just decided to let him think that.

Sophie yanked the rubber patch out of the horse's tummy. Then she shook the bank—hard—so all the money fell out.

"One, two, three . . ."

First Sophie counted all the dollars. They were mostly from her grandparents. For her birthday they always gave her as many dollars as her age. And since she had not spent that year's dollars yet, there were at least eight of them.

There were also some dollars from the tooth fairy. Plus tons of coins. Sophie added them all up.

Nineteen dollars and forty-nine cents—pretty good.

Then she added the fifty dollars.

That came to $69.49!

Sophie pushed a loose tooth with her tongue. As soon as it came out, the tooth fairy could leave her another dollar. Or maybe even two.

Sophie could not believe it. She was even richer than she had thought!

Plus she was a very good adder, which a zillionaire should be, for sure.

Sophie started to count her money one more time, just to make sure she hadn't missed any.

That was when Hayley walked in.

"What are you doing?" she asked Sophie.

"Counting my money. That's what zillionaires do," Sophie said. It was a fact.

"There is no such number as a zillion," Hayley said. She sounded bored. But she looked a tiny bit interested. "Hey, how much do you *have*?" she asked.

Sophie sat up very straight. "Sixty-nine dollars and forty-nine cents," she said.

CHEER
GO TEAM!

"Really?" Hayley sounded impressed. This made Sophie even happier. "How did you get that much?"

Sophie told her all about the fifty dollars.

"Wow! So I guess you won't mind giving me all your pennies," Hayley said.

Sophie's eyebrows bunched together. "What are you talking about?"

"My class is collecting pennies all week to help kids. They're going to build schools in parts of the world where kids don't have them," Hayley said.

"They're going to build schools out of pennies?" Sophie asked. That sounded like a silly plan.

"No, the pennies will *pay* for it," Hayley said, rolling her eyes.

"They will?" Sophie said. That plan did not sound much better. What could a penny pay for? Not even a brick, she bet.

Then Hayley explained that one penny was not much, but a whole bunch could add up to a lot of money.

"Other schools all over the state are collecting them, too. Last year they raised more than twenty thousand dollars!" Hayley said.

Twenty thousand dollars! Sophie thought.

She looked down at her piles of dollars and coins. Then she sighed, scooped the pennies up, and handed all nineteen to her sister.

"Thanks!" Hayley said, giving her a big smile.

"You're welcome," Sophie told her. And she meant it, too. She was glad Hayley had her brown pennies. Her money looked much more silvery and pretty without them, she thought.

Then she thought about the kids who would have to go to school—because of her.

Hmm. Now that Sophie was a zillionaire, she would have to make it up to them somehow.

The next day at school, Sophie had some questions for her classmates.

"How much money do you have?" she asked Mia and Eve. They were hanging up their jackets. Sophie tried very hard not to smile too big.

"I don't know," Eve said, shrugging.

"Me neither," Mia said. "Maybe twenty dollars?"

"Oh," Sophie said. Now her smile was *very* big. "Well, guess what? I have sixty-nine dollars!"

"Really?" Eve said.

Sophie nodded. "And thirty cents!" she added. "I am very, very rich!"

Then Sydney and Grace walked up to the row of cubbies.

"How much money do *you* have?" Sophie asked them.

Grace frowned. "My dad says it's not polite to ask that."

"Oh, you can tell *me*. We're friends," Sophie said.

Grace shrugged. "I'm not sure. Why do you want to know?" she asked.

Sophie stood up a little straighter. "I am glad you asked! It's just that I found fifty dollars yesterday, and I'm pretty sure that makes me the richest kid in the class! Maybe the whole school!" she said.

"How do you know?" Mia asked.

Sophie shrugged. "Well, I know we don't have any princes or princesses here," she said. "Who else has that much money?"

"Hang on," Grace said. She held up her hand to stop Sophie. "You found fifty dollars?" She looked like maybe she did not believe her.

Sophie stuck her lip out and nodded hard. "I did! Really!" Then she turned to Kate, who was taking homework out of her backpack. "Tell her, Kate. Didn't I?"

Kate looked up. "Yep, she did." She crossed her heart. "Right there on the sidewalk. Fifty whole bucks."

Sophie grinned. Thank goodness for Kate. "See!" she told everyone.

"Wow. You really are rich," Eve said. She sounded even more impressed than Hayley had been.

"I know!" Sophie did not mean to be a show-off. But she guessed that when you were very rich, you couldn't help showing off sometimes. "Just call me Sophie the Zillionaire from now on!" she said.

Sophie took a deep breath. She looked at her friends and waited for her great new name to sink in.

"But I thought you wanted us to call you Sophie the Honest," Sydney said after a minute.

"How about Sophie the Hero? What about that?" Mia asked.

Oh, right. Those other names. She had almost forgotten about them. Yes, Sophie had thought they would be good. But that was before—before she had $69.30!

Sophie waved her hand. "Forget about that. Besides, zillionaires can change their minds," she told them.

That was when Sophie A. walked up. She was the other Sophie in room 10. "You know that a zillion isn't a real number, right?" she asked.

Sophie wanted to answer, "It is real enough." But then snooty Mindy VonBoffmann walked up, too, before Sophie could say anything.

Mindy was with Lily Lemley, her best friend. Mindy handed her jacket to Lily. Lily hung it up on Mindy's hook.

"What are you all talking about?" Mindy asked them.

"Yeah. What are you talking about?" Lily echoed. She fixed her headband. It matched Mindy's exactly. It always did.

"Sophie found fifty dollars!" Mia told them.

"She's not honest anymore. She's rich!" Sydney added.

Sophie smiled and took a deep breath. She let the good feeling inside her spread. At last! She was special.

She almost said, "Actually, I'm Sophie the Zillionaire."

But just then, Mindy wrinkled her nose and curled her lip. "*Fifty* dollars?"

Sophie's good feeling bubbled up. This was getting even better! Mindy VonBoffmann was jealous! Of her! How cool was that?

Mindy looked at Lily. She raised her eyebrow and they both laughed.

"Fifty dollars is nothing. My grandmother just gave me a hundred dollars for college," Mindy said. Then she fluffed her curly blond hair.

"Don't tell my grandmother, but I'm going to buy a cell phone with it instead."

The bubbles inside Sophie popped and fizzed away.

She could not believe it. *A hundred dollars?* There was just one thing to say.

Sophie put her hands on her hips. "I don't believe it."

She knew that everyone was looking at her. But she didn't care.

(Well, okay, she kind of did.)

"Fine," Mindy said. She shrugged. "Lily, hand me my backpack."

Lily took Mindy's backpack off her own shoulder. She unzipped it and passed it to her. Mindy reached into it and moved her hand around. Then she reached in deeper and frowned.

Aha! Sophie thought. Mindy did not have a hundred dollars. She knew it. All along.

But Mindy did not stop looking in her backpack. Instead, she started to pull things out.

Things like an extra headband, and a hair-brush, and some little white cards.

"Here. Take one," Mindy told the girls.

"What are they?" Mia asked.

"My parents' business cards," Mindy said. Sophie could tell she was trying to sound grown-up and important as she handed them out.

Sophie read one:

> KEN & CINDY VONBOFFMANN
>
> —
>
> NEW & USED CARS
> LET US MAKE YOU A DEAL!

Then Mindy pulled out a picture of a pretty lady. She had a big smile and a sash that read "Miss America." And a very, very tall crown. A fancy name was signed across the bottom. Plus lots of *X*s and *O*s.

Mindy handed the picture to Lily. "Be careful with that," she said.

Lily took it very gently with both hands. "I will," she said.

Sophie rolled her eyes.

Then Mindy pulled out a little blue notebook. Her name was written on the front in gold. She smiled a tight Mindy smile. "Here it is!"

"That's not a hundred dollars," Sophie said. She crossed her arms.

This time, Mindy rolled her eyes. "Of course it's not. I keep my money in the bank. This is my passbook," she said.

Oh . . . Sophie did not know what a passbook was. So she was happy when Mia asked.

"It's how I keep track of my money, of course," Mindy explained, as if everyone should know that.

Then she opened the book and pointed to the number one hundred. It was typed in, along with a period and two zeros. Sophie knew that those stood for cents.

XOXO

Mindy grinned. Her eyes got squinty. "Need more proof? I can have my grandmother write me a note, if you want," she said.

Sophie sighed. "That's okay." She shook her head.

She was very glad that the lights flashed three times right then.

"Hang up those coats, class," Ms. Moffly, their teacher, called. "It's time to get to work."

Sophie walked over and slumped in her seat. Ms. Moffly was right: Sophie did have to get to work. She could not call herself Sophie the Zillionaire when Mindy had more money than she did.

Still, that did not mean she couldn't be a zillionaire. Not if she really, really tried. . . .

Somehow, Sophie had to turn $69.30 into more than a hundred. And fast!

☆ ☆ ☆

"I'm so excited! Aren't you?" Kate said to Sophie as they walked home from the bus stop.

Sophie shrugged. "Not really."

She was staring at the sidewalk, hoping to find fifty more dollars. Or twenty. Or ten. Or even five.

But all she'd found so far was an old, rusty barrette.

"What do you mean 'not really'? I thought riding horses was your lifelong dream," Kate said.

Sophie stopped. She looked up at Kate. "Oh, that! Of course!" she said.

She had been thinking so hard about money she'd almost forgotten their big plans. The next day they were going to ride horses!

"Yes! I am super-excited about that," Sophie said. She had been waiting for that day for almost a week now.

Still, Sophie could not help sighing.

"I just wish I could be Sophie the Zillionaire, too," she said.

"Why can't you?" Kate asked.

Sophie frowned. "Because Mindy has a hundred

whole dollars. And I have less." That was the truth.

Kate thought hard. "Why don't you just ask your grandparents to give you money? Like Mindy's did," she suggested.

Sophie stopped for a second. Her grandparents were great. But they thought eight dollars for her eighth birthday was a lot.

(If only she were turning thirty. But that was forever away!)

Sophie shook her head. "Even if my grandparents won the lottery, they would never give me that much," she said.

Hang on! Sophie thought. What had she just said?

She grabbed Kate's hand. "That's it! I know what I'll do! I'll make money the old-fashioned way!" she said.

"How?" Kate asked. Her eyes were big.

Sophie swung her hand high in the air. "I'll win the lottery!"

CHAPTER 3

When Sophie got home, she ran to her room. She got down her horse bank and counted her money again. There was still $69.30. She poked her finger around inside, just in case some money was stuck. She even peeked in with a flashlight. But no. There was no extra money. Oh, well.

Sophie started to put the bank back on her shelf. Then she stopped.

There was a lot of money in that bank. Not a hundred dollars (*yet*). But it was all the money she had in the world. And anyone could get it off her shelf. Her family never really messed with her stuff. She wasn't worried about them. But what about robbers?!

Sure, they might not know the horse was a bank. It was a good disguise. But it was so pretty they might take it, anyway.

Sophie needed to find a safer place for her bank. But where?

Maybe under her bed? Yes! It was perfect! There was so much dust and old junk no robber would ever look there.

Sophie got down on her knees. She lifted the bed skirt. Then she slid the bank underneath.

There! Her money already seemed safer. She patted her polka-dot bedspread and grinned.

Of course, Sophie bet that when she won the lottery, her money would not all fit in her horse bank. It might not all even fit under her bed. She would probably have to take it to a real bank, like Mindy did. She would miss it then.

Sophie decided to tell her parents about her great lottery idea that night at dinner. She was ready as soon as they sat down. Dinner was always pretty quick, because Max did not stay in his high chair for long.

"Mmm! This looks good," her dad said.

They were having spaghetti with meat sauce. Sophie liked meatballs better, but Max thought all balls were for throwing. They would probably never have meatballs again.

"Thank you!" Sophie's mom said. She put a plate in front of Max. Then she sat down quickly and turned to Hayley. "How's the penny drive coming?" she asked.

Hayley was sprinkling parmesan cheese all over her plate. "Great! We have six pounds already," she said.

Six pounds? Really? Sophie did not know you could count money that way. *How many pounds do I have?* she wondered.

She also wondered when Hayley would be done with the cheese.

"Hey," Sophie said. "Save some for me."

Her mom gave her a look.

Sophie smiled at her sister. "*Please*."

Hayley slid the cheese over.

There was not a lot left. But that was okay, Sophie guessed. When she won the lottery, she would buy at least six pounds of it.

Oh, right. The lottery!

"Hey, Dad. I have a question," Sophie said. "Can you take me to get a lottery ticket? Tonight? *Please?*"

Her dad chuckled and shook his head. "Sorry, Sophie. You have to be eighteen to buy a lottery ticket, I'm afraid," he said.

"You do?" Sophie said.

That was no fair! Why were grown-ups the only ones who could get rich easily?

"Why do you want a lottery ticket, anyway?" Hayley asked, twirling some spaghetti on her fork.

"I need to make more money. Fast," Sophie said. She turned back to her dad and shrugged. "I guess you'll have to buy one for me."

Sophie's mom gave her a look. Again.

"*Please!*" Sophie grinned.

But her mom just shook her head. "We are not buying you a lottery ticket, Sophie," she said. She sounded very sure. And a little grumpy. "Do you know what your chances of winning are?"

"No," Sophie said. She did not.

"About one in a zillion," her mom said.

"You know, a zillion is not a real number," Hayley chimed in.

Sophie rolled her eyes. "All *I* know is that you have to play to win," she said.

Sophie's mom reached over to Max. She pulled a noodle out of his nose. Then she turned back to Sophie. "What gave you *that* idea?" she asked.

Sophie shrugged. She pointed to her dad.

His mouth was full. So he made a "who, me?" face. Then he swallowed.

"Who, me?" he said.

"Yes, you. You always say that when we win the lottery, we'll buy a new TV. Or a new car. And every time Mom says, 'In your dreams,' you say, 'You have to play to win!'" Sophie said.

"No, I do not," said her dad.

Hayley nodded. "Yes, you do," she told him.

Now Sophie's mom rolled her eyes. "That's just the way Daddy talks. We both know that the lottery is a much better way to lose money than to make it, right?" She looked at him.

"Um, yes," he said.

But he didn't sound like he meant it. Not to Sophie, anyway.

Sophie's mom turned back to her. "Do you know what the best way to get money is?" she asked.

Sophie could think of only one other way. "Find it?"

Her mom sighed. "No. Earn it."

Earn it? *Hmm.* That sounded more like the *hard* way than the best way to Sophie.

"Maybe it's time to start giving you an allowance, like Hayley," Sophie's mom went on. "That means you have to do chores around the house, of course."

"Okay," Sophie said.

"You could help do the dishes," Sophie's mom

continued. "And take out the trash. Or—oh!" She looked down at the pile of noodles under Max's chair. "You could clean up after Max!"

Sophie looked down, too. *Yuck!* "How much would you pay me?" she asked.

"Let's see. How about four dollars a week?" her mom said.

Four dollars? A week?

"That's *it*?" Sophie frowned.

Just then, Max tossed his dish onto the floor. Sophie's mom looked down at the mess.

She turned back to Sophie. "Okay. Five dollars," she said.

Sophie nodded. It was better than nothing, she guessed. But five dollars a week was not going to make her a zillionaire fast. She still needed to make more money some other way, too.

She tried to think of how . . . but the idea did not come to her right then.

And it did not come while she was scooping Max's dinner into a dustpan, either. *Gross!*

(What came to her then was this: When Sophie

was a zillionaire, the first thing she would do was pay someone else to clean up after Max!)

But the idea *did* come to her later, when her mom put out dessert: cupcakes from a bake sale at the high school where Sophie's dad had fixed computers that day.

"The seniors were raising money to help pay for a trip to New York City," her dad said.

Right away, Sophie was paying attention.

"How much did they make?" she asked. She tried to sound casual.

Her dad shrugged. "I don't know. . . . A lot."

A lot? That was how much Sophie needed. Exactly!

That was it—she would have a bake sale!

CHAPTER 4

The next day was Saturday. That was a great day for a bake sale!

Except that it wasn't. Because that was the day Sophie and her friends were going to Mrs. Belle's daughter's horse farm. Of course!

Mrs. Belle was Kate's babysitter. She had her own kids, but they were grown up. And now one of them had a horse farm. With real, live horses. To ride on!

Kate was allowed to bring her five best friends: Sophie and Eve and Mia and Sydney and Grace. They were going to ride horses.

Sophie was sorry they could not sleep over. That had been the plan. But that plan had changed when Kate asked to invite more friends. Still! They were riding horses. And Sophie could hardly wait!

Sophie's dad dropped her off at the farm in the morning. Right away, she saw Kate standing with a grown-up outside the barn. Both of them waved as Sophie walked up.

"This is my friend Sophie," Kate said.

"Hey, there! I'm Mrs. Belle's daughter, Tallulah. Welcome to Blue-Belle Farms," said the grown-up.

Sophie stared. Mrs. Belle's daughter did not look like Mrs. Belle. At all.

Mrs. Belle had very short, very blond hair. It was also very curly.

Tallulah had a thick ponytail. Her hair was long and brown and straight.

Mrs. Belle wore very pink lipstick. And very tight pantsuits. Most times they were very bright.

Tallulah did not have on lipstick. She had on jeans. They were torn and loose and very light.

Sophie would never have thought that they were related. She did not say this, though.

What she did say was "Nice to meet you. I'm Sophie the Z—"

But she did not get to finish. By then, Tallulah had turned around.

"Come check out the barn!" Tallulah called over her shoulder.

"Come on, Sophie the Zillionaire!" said Kate.

Sophie grinned. Together, they followed Tallulah into the big barn.

Grace and Sydney were waiting inside. Sophie was not surprised. She was never the first—or the last—to get anywhere. But maybe she would be when she was a zillionaire. Instead of her dad, a chauffeur could drive her. And she could buy a car that was long . . . and very fast.

But she would worry about that later. Right now, she had horses to ride!

She was happy when Eve and Mia walked in.

"Hey! Everyone's here. Can we see the horses now?" Sophie asked.

"Hay is for horses." Tallulah laughed. "But you bet we can!"

She led them to a row of stalls. Sophie grinned and held her breath. She grinned because she was excited. She held her breath because of the smell.

She sure hoped they were going to ride outside. It was kind of stinky in there.

Then, all of a sudden, Sophie's heart knocked her breath loose. She forgot about the smell.

A long black face poked through a stall door. It was looking right at her!

"This is Prince," said Tallulah. She reached up and rubbed the horse's nose.

Prince! That was perfect. *What a great name for a zillionaire's horse,* Sophie thought.

She waved her hand. "Can I ride him?" she asked.

Tallulah patted his neck. It looked strong and

smooth. "Have you ridden before?" she asked Sophie.

Sophie shook her head. "But it is my lifelong dream!" she said.

Tallulah smiled. "Mine, too. But Prince here is a handful. I have some ponies who would be much better for you," she said.

Ponies? Sophie was not sure she liked the sound of that. Her dream was to ride big beautiful horses. Not little ponies.

Then Tallulah turned to the other girls. "Has anyone ridden before?" she asked.

Sophie looked around. She really hoped not! Sophie the Zillionaire should not be riding a little pony when everyone else had a big horse.

Luckily, the girls all said no.

Phew.

Tallulah led them to another row of stalls. Over the doors, Sophie saw signs with the horses' names painted on them.

There were Sinbad . . . and Ringo . . . and

Joker . . . and Daisy . . . and Penny . . . and Duchess . . .

Duchess! That would work! A duchess was kind of like a prince—or a princess. Sophie was pretty sure, anyway.

She almost said, "I'll take that one!"

Only, before she could, Mrs. Belle's daughter gave Duchess to Grace!

"Here, Sophie. You take Penny," Tallulah said. "She'll be perfect for you."

Penny? Perfect? Sophie the Zillionaire did not think so.

She cleared her throat. "Um, do you think I could have Duchess instead? You might not know this," she said softly—she did not want the other girls to feel bad—"but I have a fifty-dollar bill at home. I'm almost the richest kid in my class. So a horse named Penny doesn't seem right."

"I see," said Tallulah. She turned to Penny's stall. A reddish brown face was peeking out. It nodded two times. Then it blew and made a soft, shivery horse sound.

"Too bad," Tallulah went on. "I think Penny really likes you."

Really? Penny liked her?

The pony nodded again.

"Do you still want to switch?" Tallulah asked her.

"No, that's okay." Sophie shook her head. Tallulah was right. Penny did like her. And she liked Penny, too, now.

Plus Penny was not a small pony at all. She was big. Much bigger than Sophie. So big, Sophie wondered how she would ever get up on her back.

"Is there a ladder?" she asked Tallulah. "I'm ready to go!"

"Yeah!" cheered the other girls. They were ready, too!

But they learned that this was not how it worked.

They learned that before you rode a horse or a pony, you had to groom it. And that meant lots of brushing—which was fun.

It also meant cleaning the pony's feet—which

was hard if he didn't want to pick them up (like Kate's pony, Joker).

Joker whinnied as Kate kept trying.

"He's laughing at me," Kate groaned.

They also learned that before you rode, you and your pony both had to dress up. The pony had to put on a bridle and a blanket. Oh, and a saddle. Of course. The riders had to put on hard hats. They were a lot like helmets, but very plain. (Sophie decided when she was a zillionaire, she would buy a fancy one.)

Then the riding part came. Finally! That was when the girls learned other things.

Things like:

You didn't use a ladder to get on the pony. You used a big box called a mounting block, instead. And you always got on from the pony's left side. And you had to be fast, or he would walk off.

Also, the ground looked really far away from the top of a pony! Sophie was glad to be wearing her hard hat then. She did not care at all that it was plain.

Once the girls were on their ponies, they rode around a ring. Kate got to be first. Sophie was in the middle, as usual. But that was fine with her. Steering a pony was not easy.

"Just follow Ringo," Sophie whispered in Penny's tall ear.

And she did. The whole time. Penny was such a smart pony!

Then they learned that an hour of riding went fast. Even when you were just riding around . . . and around . . . and around.

And all that grooming you did before you rode? You had to do it all over again after.

And they also learned that there were pony treats—like dog treats, but much bigger. And that pony teeth were big, too. And that pony drool was not too bad. (Pony poop, though, kind of was.)

And Sophie learned one more thing. This was probably the most important: A horse's name did not matter. They were all great, no matter what!

In fact, Sophie knew what she would buy before a fancy hard hat or a fast car when she was a real zillionaire: a horse farm and lots of ponies just like Penny.

And lots of air freshener, too!

Sophie had more reasons than ever to be a zillionaire now. She had to buy all those things. And pay someone to do her chores. And she had to have more money than Mindy VonBoffmann, of course.

Sophie did not think the first thing could happen before Monday. Pony farms were pricey, she bet.

But the next two things might happen fast—if her bake sale went well.

Sophie told Kate about her amazing bake sale idea as Kate's mom drove them home from the farm.

Kate wanted to help. "But if I help, do I get to make some money, too?" Kate asked.

Sophie thought about this for a second. Kate had a good point.

Plus if Kate made her own money, Sophie would not have to buy her gum. Kate could buy it herself.

Sophie grinned and shook Kate's hand. "We are now business partners!" she said.

CHAPTER 5

On Sunday afternoon, Kate came over.

"So, what are we baking?" she asked.

Sophie smiled. What else? "What is the all-time best-ever bake sale treat?" she said.

Kate rubbed her hands together. Her eyes got very big. She licked her lips and smiled back at Sophie. "Rice Krispies Treats!"

Huh? No. Sophie shook her head.

"Chocolate chip cookies!" she said.

Kate's eyes got normal again. "Oh. Are you sure?" she asked.

"Sure I'm sure. Besides, I already made a sign," Sophie said.

She held up a big piece of cardboard she'd found in the garage. She had written big words on it in Magic Marker.

BAKE SALE TODAY!
CHOCKLIT CHIP COOKEES!
#5 – CHEEP!

Kate scratched a freckle on her chin. "Are you sure you wrote that right?" she asked.

Sophie studied her sign. "Maybe that's not the way you spell 'chocolate.' But it's close enough," she said.

Kate shook her head. "I don't mean that. I mean the price. Five dollars for one cookie?"

"Well, yeah!" Sophie nodded hard. "Don't you want to make as much money as we can?" she asked.

Kate shrugged. "I guess so. It just seems like a lot," she said.

Sophie looked at the sign. *Hmm.* Maybe Kate was right. Maybe that was a lot. For one regular cookie.

So she added two words.

DEELISHUS!

and

SPESHUL!

"Better?" Sophie asked Kate.

Kate grinned. "Yes," she said. "Uh . . . but are you sure you spelled *those* right?"

"Who cares?" Sophie waved her hand. That was not important when there were cookies to make!

The girls headed into the kitchen. Sophie put on an apron. She gave Kate one, too.

Then Sophie pulled out her cookbook. It was the one just for kids. She turned past the Stone Soup. And the Easy-Cheesy Carrots and Peasies. But she stopped at the World's Best Rocko-Chocko Chips.

Yes!

"Okay," Sophie said. "We need some butter. . . ." She opened the fridge.

Just then, her mom walked in.

"Guess what? Dad took Max to the playground. So I'm all yours. How can I help?" she asked.

Sophie waved her mom out of the room. "You can't," she said.

Her mom looked surprised. "Are you sure?"

"I am very sure," Sophie said.

She was very sure that she and Kate could make the cookies all by themselves. And she was very sure she that she did not want to split the profits with anyone else. Not even her mom.

"Okay . . . ," her mom said. She used that voice that sounded like she did not really mean it. "But call me when it's oven time. You girls do need help with that."

"Fine," Sophie said, blowing her bangs off her forehead.

She rolled her eyes as her mom left.

"Moms," she and Kate both said.

Then they got baking.

They mixed everything the book said to mix, step by step by step. They also mixed in some eggshells. (That was an accident. They got them out, mostly.) Then all they needed were chocolate chips!

"Hey!" Sophie said, poking all around the pantry.

"Hay is for horses," Kate joked.

"No, hey is for 'Where are the chocolate chips?!'" Sophie said.

She poked around some more. Kate poked, too. Where could they be?

Sophie checked all the cabinets. And the drawers. And the fridge. But there was not even one chocolate chip!

"What do we do?" Sophie cried.

"Well . . . I guess we could put in something else," Kate said. "Do you have any other kind of chips?"

Sophie shook her head. She did not.

She guessed she could use some of her money to buy more chocolate chips at the store. But she really did not want to.

One thing was for sure: When Sophie was a

real zillionaire, she would always keep chocolate chips around. A whole cabinet full!

"I know! How about we put in gum?" Kate suggested.

Sophie shook her head again. "I don't have any. And besides, you'd have to keep chewing the cookies forever then. That might be sort of gross."

"We should have made Rice Krispies Treats, I guess," Kate said.

Sophie started to sigh. But then she stopped. "Hey!"

"Hay is for—" Kate said. But Sophie held up her hand.

"Horses. I know," Sophie said. She grinned. "But listen to this. We know Rice Krispies are good in treats. Do you think they'd be good in cookies?"

"Yes!" Kate's eyes lit up.

They ran to the pantry and grabbed the cereal box. They dumped a few Rice Krispies into the dough. Then they dumped in a lot. Then they

RICE CEREAL
yum
OIL
BAKING SODA
SA
FLOUR

stirred and stirred until they couldn't feel their arms anymore.

"Are you thinking what I'm thinking?" Kate asked.

"I think so," said Sophie. "It's oven time, Mom!"

☆ ☆ ☆

While the cookies baked, Sophie fixed her sign. She crossed out CHOCKLIT CHIP and wrote RICE KRISPEE. And she added TOP SECRET RESSIPY across the top.

She tried to taste one cookie right out of the oven. It was so hot that it burned her tongue. *Ouch!*

She waited for another to cool. Kate did, too. Then they tried again. *Yum!* The Rice Krispies were good! Sophie missed the chocolate chips, but not as much as she thought she would.

They piled the cookies high on a plate.

"Ready to make some money?" Sophie asked.

"You bet!" Kate said.

Kate grabbed the plate, and Sophie grabbed

the sign and an empty baby wipes box. That was for keeping the money they made in. She hoped it was big enough.

Their plan was to get the folding table from the garage. They would set it up on the sidewalk out front and sell and sell until every single delicious cookie was gone.

But before they got to the door, Sophie's dad came in with Max. Sophie stopped and stared at them. They looked like they'd been swimming—in their clothes!

"It's raining cats and dogs out there!" Sophie's dad said. Then he shook his hair. A puddle was forming under him. Max jumped down and splashed around.

Sophie's jaw fell. *No, no, no!* It could not rain! Not now! Not on her bake sale!

"No, no, no! It can't rain! Not now! Not on my bake sale!" she cried.

"Sorry, Sophie," her dad said. "I think that will have to wait now."

He took off his coat. Then he sniffed. "Mmm,

smells good!" He grinned. "Hey, can I have a cookie?"

"Hay is for horses. But yes," Kate said. She held the plate out.

Sophie's dad reached for it. But Sophie quickly stopped him. She held up her sign. "That will be five dollars, please!"

Her dad's jaw fell open this time.

"Five *dollars*? For one cookie? That seems like a lot," he said.

Sophie shrugged. "It's for a good cause, Dad," she said.

"Really? What?" he asked.

Sophie raised her chin. "So I can be a zillionaire!"

"And so I can buy gum," Kate added, smiling wide. She held out the cookie plate again.

Sophie waited for her dad to take out his wallet. But his wallet stayed in his pocket. "I might have to think about this," he said, rubbing his chin.

But Max did not have to think. He just grabbed a cookie in each hand. Then he ran.

"Hey! That will be ten dollars!" Sophie yelled after him.

☆ ☆ ☆

Sophie had really hoped to make a zillion dollars at her bake sale. Or at least another fifty. But that did not happen.

She and Kate still set up their bake sale table. But they set it up inside, in Sophie's front hall.

And they waited. And waited. And waited.

Sophie had hoped the mailman, or a neighbor, or even her Aunt Maggie would stop by.

But then she remembered that it was Sunday. The mailman did not work. And Aunt Maggie went out to eat with the other old ladies at her church.

At least her dad bought one cookie. Finally. After she let him "test-drive" some.

Soon it was time for Kate to go home. Sophie counted up what they had: one five-dollar bill in the wipes box and two aches in their tummies. One for each of them.

Sophie wished they had sold more cookies. And eaten fewer.

"I guess there's just one thing to do," she told Kate. Then she stood up. "Going-out-of-business sale! Everything must go!" she yelled.

Sophie's mom popped out of the kitchen. "I'll give you ten dollars for the whole plate," she said.

Kate held her stomach and nodded.

"Deal," Sophie said.

That meant fifteen dollars total. Seven fifty for her, and seven fifty for Kate.

Kate was happy. She could buy lots of gum.

But Sophie was not. $69.30 plus her $5.00 allowance plus $7.50 equaled $81.80.

Sure, it was better. But it was still not enough to make Sophie a zillionaire!

By Monday morning, Sophie still had $81.80. (Her loose tooth had not fallen out yet. *Sigh.*)

Plus it was still raining. And her left rain boot was missing. But at least her stomachache was gone.

If only Sophie were richer than Mindy already. It was hard to wait to be special. She wanted to be special right now!

Sophie wondered if she was rich enough, at least, to buy a new pair of rain boots. Her sneakers were all squishy by the time she got to school.

In room 10, she hung up her raincoat. Lily had just hung up Mindy's coat for her.

"How does Mindy get her to do all that stuff?" Kate whispered to Sophie. "You so couldn't pay me to!"

I know, Sophie thought. Then, suddenly, she froze.

Hang on!

Getting paid to do things for people? She could do that! Why not?

Sophie looked at the other kids walking into the classroom. She thought about what Hayley had said about a little money adding up to a lot.

There were twenty-four kids in Sophie's class. What if she could make a dollar from every one of them?

She did the math. (That was another thing about being rich that was fun.) If she added $24.00 to her $81.80, she'd have more than a hundred dollars. Way more!

But wait. She couldn't count herself. Of course. And she couldn't count Kate, either. So that was not as much. But it was still more than a hundred. . . .

What am I waiting for? Sophie thought.

She ran up to Ben as he walked through the door. "Hi, Ben!" she said.

"Hi, Sophie," Ben answered. He looked very happy to talk to her. And a little surprised, too.

"Can I hang up your coat for you?" Sophie asked.

"Uh, sure . . . ," Ben said. He looked even more surprised as he passed his coat over.

"Great!" Sophie took his drippy raincoat in one hand. "That will be one dollar," she said, holding out her other hand.

Ben looked a lot surprised now. "A dollar? For what?"

"For hanging up your coat," Sophie said. She smiled at him, really big.

But Ben frowned at her. "You never said anything about having to pay."

Oops. Sophie had forgotten that part. But why else did Ben think she would hang up his coat?

"Sorry," she said. "You're my first customer."

But Ben took back his coat. "I don't think so," he said, shaking his head.

Sophie sighed. She watched Ben walk off. But she wasn't going to give up. Zillionaires never gave up!

So she went over to Sophie A.

And Eve.

And Dean.

And Mia.

And Jack.

But they did not want to pay her to hang up their coats, either.

Or shake out their umbrellas.

Or tie their wet shoelaces.

Or pull out their chairs.

Or sharpen their pencils.

Sophie could not believe it!

There was only one person who offered to pay her. That person was Toby Myers.

"I'll give you a dollar to pick Archie's nose," he said.

Sophie shot him a look.

"No way! I like to pick my own nose!" Archie declared.

Boys! *Gross!*

Still, Sophie kept trying.

"I'll pick out a book for you. For a dollar," she said to Sydney later in the library.

Sydney frowned. She shook her head.

"Fifty cents?" Sophie said.

Sydney's head kept shaking.

"How about a quarter?" Sophie asked. She tried to look super-helpful, like a great book-picker-outer.

"Why would I pay you to do something that I like to do myself?" Sydney finally asked.

Hmm. Sydney had a point. Maybe Sophie had a better chance of making money if she offered to do things that people *hated* doing.

Sophie picked out her own library book and thought about that a little more.

She was still thinking back in room 10 as Ms. Moffly wrote on the board. The teacher was writing vocabulary words for the class to copy later.

They were supposed to write in their journals first. But Sophie's journal page was still blank. She leaned on her hand. Sure, she had things to write about. But all she could think about was being Sophie the Zillionaire.

"Has anybody paid you yet?" Kate whispered, leaning over.

"No. Not yet," Sophie told her. "But if I could just think of something that nobody wants to do . . ."

Kate pointed to the blackboard. Ms. Moffly had a made a *looong* list. "Like copying vocabulary words," Kate groaned.

"Hey!" Sophie suddenly said.

"Hay is for horses!" Kate said back.

"No! Hey is for 'That's what I can do to make money!'" Sophie said.

It was perfect! The class had the rest of the day to copy their vocabulary words. That meant Sophie had plenty of time to put her plan into action!

She started by asking Grace and Sydney. It was easy. They sat at her table.

"Hey, Grace. Hey, Sydney," she whispered. "I'll make you a deal. I'll write down your vocabulary words . . . for a small fee." That sounded very professional, she knew. She'd heard it on a real commercial.

"You want us to pay you?" Grace stared at Sophie. It was like Sophie had asked to cut off her head.

But Sydney slowly rubbed her chin. "How much?" she asked.

Good question, Sophie thought.

She looked back at the vocabulary list. Twenty-five words. *Ugh.* That was a lot!

She wanted to say, "Fifty dollars." But she guessed that was too much.

"Five dollars," she told Sydney.

"Five dollars!" Sydney said. Now it was like Sophie had asked to cut off *her* head. "How about fifty cents?"

"Four dollars?" Sophie asked, trying again.

"Seventy-five cents," Sydney said. She crossed her arms.

Sophie sighed. Sydney drove a hard bargain.

"Okay. A dollar. But that's my final offer," Sophie said.

Sydney held out her hand. "Deal."

They shook on it. *Yes!*

Then Sophie turned to Kate and smiled. If she could have winked, she would have. Maybe when she was a zillionaire, she would get that fixed.

But for now, she had a paying customer!

"Oh, okay. I'll do it, too. For a dollar," Grace said.

Oh, boy! Sophie had *two* paying customers. The money was starting to roll in!

"There's just one problem," Sydney said then. "I don't have any money with me."

"Me neither," Grace added.

Sophie frowned. So she had customers. But they were not paying. Now what?

Then Sydney did something interesting. She wrote three letters on the top of a piece of paper.

IOU
$1
Sydney

"What's this?" Sophie asked.

"It's an IOU," Sydney said. "It means I owe you a dollar. I'll give you this today and bring the money tomorrow."

"Me too!" Grace said.

Hmm . . .

Sophie guessed that was okay. And it turned out that Sydney and Grace were not the only ones who said they would hire Sophie. (*Hooray!*) And they were not the only ones who could not pay her that day. (*Oh, well.*)

By lunchtime, Sophie had twelve orders for vocabulary lists. And twelve IOUs.

She had hoped for a lot more. But there were some kids—like Sophie A.—who liked copying their own lists. And there were some kids—like Toby and Archie—who she'd rather not work for. They could copy their own lists. (And pick their own noses, for that matter.)

And then there was Mindy. She did not need a list copied, either. That was because Lily had already copied one for her. For free.

By the end of lunch, though, Sophie had decided that twelve lists was plenty. In fact, she was a little worried. What if it was too much? She had copied and copied all through lunch. Now it was time for recess, and she only had six lists done.

Sophie was a very, very fast reader. But she was a very, very slow writer.

She shook out her hand. It was sore. Her pencil was dull. And worse than that, her stomach was empty. She had not stopped to eat at all.

"Come on," said Kate. "Let's play. Haven't you written enough?"

Sophie gave a big sigh and held up a stack of blank paper. "No," she said. "I'm only half done."

So instead of playing in the gym during recess (since it was still raining), Sophie sat on the bleachers and copied *more* words.

Sophie wished she had picked something else to help her earn money. Something quick. Like cleaning out cubbies. She could have done twelve of those in no time. Oh, well. She could do that the next day. If her hand still worked.

Before Sophie knew it, recess was over. She still had three more lists to go. And that wasn't the worst part. Sophie had been so busy writing that she had missed seeing Dean's bloody nose!

"I can't believe you didn't see that!" Ben said. "He ran right into the goalpost!"

Sophie could not believe it, either. It was not every day she got to see a good bloody nose! It was all anyone could talk about.

And when Ms. Moffly said the class could play charades at the end of the day, Sophie could not believe that, either.

"*If* you don't still have to copy your vocabulary list," the teacher added.

Sophie plopped her head into her hands—for two reasons.

One was that she was the only person who still had a list to copy. And the other was that she loved charades. And she really hated to miss it.

At least by the time school was over, she had all the lists done. She passed them out to her friends. They passed their IOUs to her.

She counted them. Twelve. And she felt a little better. No, it wasn't money. But it was close.

Sophie smiled and climbed onto the bus with Kate. They walked to their favorite seat in the back. Sophie sat down. She shook the rain off her coat and rubbed her sore hand. But she forgot to scrunch down to hide from Ella Fitzgibbon . . . until it was too late.

"*SOOO-PHIE!*" called a squeaky voice. It was Ella's. Of course.

The kindergartener ran down the aisle to them and hugged Sophie. Hard. "My hero!" she said.

Sophie sighed. She couldn't help it. Ella's hug was sticky, as usual. But that day it was also drippy wet, from all the rain.

"You know, you don't have to call me that anymore, Ella," Sophie told her.

Sure, Sophie had saved Ella's life the week before. But that seemed so long ago now. Being a hero had been fun—for a while. But it was hard to keep up!

Ella plopped down in the seat across from Sophie. "Aw, but I like it!"

Kate leaned over. "Sophie's a *zillionaire* now, Ella," she said.

"Really?" Ella's eyes got big. "How much money do you have?"

Sophie sat up straight. She looked down at Ella. "Almost a hundred dollars," she said.

She waited for Ella to say, "Wow!" Or "Whoa!" Or "Oh, boy!"

But Ella just stared.

"*One* hundred dollars? Is that all?" she said.

What?

Sophie guessed that Ella had not learned big numbers, like one hundred, yet.

"That's one *hundred*. One zero zero. *Dollars*," Sophie said.

"I know what a hundred is," Ella told her. "I can count all the way there. Want to hear? One, two, three, four, five, six, sev—"

"That's okay," Sophie said.

Ella shrugged. "I bet I have a hundred hundred dollars!" the kindergartner said.

Sophie turned to Kate and made a "what is Ella talking about?" face.

Then Sophie started to get a feeling. It was cold. And it wasn't from her wet shoes.

Sophie was so close to having more money than Mindy. She was so close to being the richest girl she knew. But if little Ella had so much more money than Sophie did . . . then Sophie's great new name was never going to work!

But no! What was she worried about?

Ella was no zillionaire. Everyone knew that. Plus everyone knew that kindergartners loved to lie. (Back when she was five, Sophie had told some good ones herself.)

Sophie smiled at Kate. Her cold feeling warmed up. (But her shoes didn't.)

Then she patted Ella's hand. "Good for you, Ella. I'd love to see all that money sometime," she said.

As soon as Sophie got home, she ran to her room. She had some homework to do—like copying her own vocabulary words. Luckily, Kate had loaned Sophie her list. Sophie had been so busy copying others she had forgotten to do her own.

But she had some other important things to do first.

Sophie reached under her bed, grabbed her bank, and dumped out the money. Yep. There was still $81.80.

She added the twelve IOUs. They meant she'd have $93.80 by the next day.

Sophie did not have a hundred dollars—yet. But she was so close! And to think that a few days earlier, she'd had less than twenty dollars. If she kept making money this fast, she'd be richer than even her parents, in no time at all!

Sophie guessed her mom was right. Earning it was a pretty good way to make money. At least until she was old enough to buy a lottery ticket of her own.

And there were all kinds of things Sophie could do to earn money! But how would people know to ask her?

Hmm . . .

She could make a sign. But where would she hang it?

She could put an ad in the newspaper. But who looked at that?

No, Sophie needed something to give out to people. Something they could keep. Something like . . . business cards!

Sophie put all her money back into her bank. Then she carefully hid it under her bed again.

She pulled some paper out of her desk drawer and started to cut it into little squares.

That was not easy, though. They did not turn out very great.

Suddenly, Sophie got an idea. It was better than cutting out cards. Much!

She went into her parents' room. She looked in the nightstand. Yes!

There were her dad's business cards. They were piled up nice and straight. And there were a zillion of them!

Sophie took the whole pile back to her room. Then she got to work.

On all the backs, she wrote her own cards. They sounded good!

SOPHIE THE ZILLIONAIRE – AT YOUR SERVISS!

PAY ME TO DO STUFF SO YOU DON'T HAVE TO!
NEW AND IMPROOVED! MORE FOR YOUR MONEY!
(I TAKE IOUS)

Then Hayley walked in. She looked down at Sophie, who was sitting on the floor.

"What are you doing now?" Hayley asked.

Sophie smiled at her sister. "Have I got a deal for you!" she said, holding out a card.

Hayley rolled her eyes. She did not make a deal. But that was okay. Sophie was sure she'd make plenty of them the next day.

☆ ☆ ☆

When Sophie got to the bus stop the next morning, she showed her business cards to Kate.

Sophie was so excited! (And not just because of the money, but also because it had finally stopped raining. *Hooray!*)

"So?" Sophie grinned. "What do you think?"

Kate read the card. "I didn't know you could fix computers!" she said.

Huh?

Oh! Kate was reading Sophie's dad's side of the business card.

"No, no. Turn it over," Sophie said.

Kate did. She read the back.

"Very cool! Can I keep it?" she asked.

Sophie smiled. "Of course! You're my best friend!" Then she thought of something. "But if I run out, I might need it back. . . ."

"No problem," Kate said, linking arms with Sophie.

The bus came rolling down the street. When it stopped, the kids climbed on.

"Good morning!" said Mrs. Blatt, the bus driver.

"Good morning!" Sophie said. She handed the bus driver one of her cards.

Mrs. Blatt read it carefully. "Well, well, well! Sophie the Zillionaire, is it?" she said.

Sophie nodded. "That's me!" she said.

She wondered what Mrs. Blatt might need her to do? Pump some gas? Fill up her tires? But before she could ask, a squeaky voice called out, "Sophie! Look what I got!"

Sophie knew who it was without turning around. But she turned, anyway. And that was when she saw it.

Ella was running up to the bus with her hands full . . . of *money!*

Sophie could not believe it!

When Ella got to the bus, she was panting. She climbed up the steps. "Hi, Mrs. Blatt! Hey, Sophie! Look!"

And that was when Sophie saw something else.

Ella's money was not just green. It was lots of colors.

Sophie turned to Kate and they both giggled. And Sophie sighed a little, too.

Ella's hands were full of *Monopoly* money.

Phew!

☆ ☆ ☆

At school, Sophie hurried to hang up her jacket. Then she took out her IOUs. She stood by the door just as Sydney walked into the room.

Sophie waved to her. "Morning!" she called.

"Morning, Sophie," Sydney said.

"So, did you bring in the dollar?" Sophie asked.

Sydney cocked her head. "Huh?"

Sophie held up her IOU.

"Oh, right!" Sydney nodded. Then she reached into her backpack and pulled out a dollar. She handed it over. "Here you go."

Sophie took the dollar and grinned. Her first dollar of the day!

"Thanks!" she said. Then she reached into her pocket and handed Sydney one of her cards. "Call me if you need anything else done for you!"

Sydney read the card. "I didn't know you could fix computers," she said.

Sophie groaned. She should have crossed her dad's side out, she guessed.

She almost took the card back to do it. But more kids were coming in. She would have to fix her cards later. Right now she had more IOUs to collect.

Soon she had a whole pile of dollars.

Only one person so far forgot. Jack.

Then there was Grace. She did not forget. She just wouldn't pay.

She showed Sophie her vocabulary list. "I can't read your writing, Sophie!" she said.

Grace had a point. Sophie could not read it, either.

"Sorry," Sophie said. She must have been tired by the time she copied Grace's list.

After that, there was just one more kid to collect from—Dean.

Sophie took out his IOU. Then she walked up to him.

Dean held out a five-dollar bill. He looked a little sad. "This is all I have. I didn't want to spend it. But I guess I have to," he said.

"Don't worry. I have plenty of change," Sophie said.

She took the five-dollar bill and counted four dollars to give back.

Then she felt a warm hand on her shoulder.

"What is going on here?" Ms. Moffly asked.

Sophie turned to see her teacher. Ms. Moffly was staring at her. And she looked surprised.

"Hi, Ms. Moffly! Not too much is going on. I'm just getting money from Dean," Sophie said.

"Excuse me?" said Ms. Moffly. She still looked surprised. But now she looked confused, too. "You can't take money from other students, Sophie. Especially not in school."

Huh?

"Oh . . . no!" Sophie got it. Ms. Moffly did not understand. "I'm not *taking* money. I earned it!" she explained.

Sophie reached into her pocket. She pulled out one of her cards, turned it Sophie–side up, and handed it to Ms. Moffly.

"I have a business," she went on. "I'm going to make lots of money! I wanted to win the lottery, but my mom thinks that earning money is a better idea. So let me know if you need something done. I have deals for kids *and* grown-ups!"

Ms. Moffly's eyes went back and forth from Sophie's card to Sophie.

At last, her eyes moved to Dean. "Would you excuse us, please?" she asked. Then Ms. Moffly held her hand out toward the door. "Let's have a talk in the hall, Sophie."

A talk. In the hall. Sophie's knees suddenly felt shaky.

She'd had talks in the hall before. For two different reasons.

One was in first grade when her teacher, Mrs. Smart, told Sophie that her mom had a new baby. The baby was Max. But that was before he had a name.

The other reason for talks in the hall was that Sophie was in big trouble. That had happened in lots of grades. Not just the first.

This day Sophie was pretty sure her mom was not having a baby. But how could she be in big trouble? She had not done anything bad. She had only copied vocabulary words.

Out in the hall, Ms. Moffly knelt down. She and Sophie were nose to nose. "First, Sophie, I want you to know that I admire your entrepreneurial spirit," she said.

Sophie stood very still. She did not know what that meant. But at least it did not sound like she was in big trouble. Yet.

"But I'm afraid that school is just not the place for it," Ms. Moffly said then. "You cannot ask other students for money. Those are the rules."

Hang on. Those were the rules? That did not seem right to Sophie.

"But what about the penny drive?" she asked Ms. Moffly. "My sister's whole class is asking for money from everyone in the school!"

Ms. Moffly shrugged. "Well, that's different," she said.

Sophie shrugged back. "How?"

"How?" Ms. Moffly repeated. She put her fingertips together. Her pink nail polish was so pretty. Sophie decided she would have to buy some, too, when she was a zillionaire.

"Well . . . ," Ms. Moffly went on. "Because the fifth grade is asking for money to help other people. Less fortunate people. Not themselves."

"Oh . . . ," Sophie said. That was a little different. Or maybe even a lot different.

She looked down at the money—the five-dollar bill and the five ones—still in her hand. She let out a little sigh.

"And you know, you'll have to return the money you took today," Ms. Moffly said.

Sophie sucked her sigh back in. "I *do*?!"

Ms. Moffly nodded. "You do," she said.

Sophie hung her head. She still was not sure if she was in big trouble. But she might as well have been.

☆ ☆ ☆

Sophie knew that giving the money back would be hard. And it was. At first. One thing was for sure: Subtracting was not as fun as adding. At all!

Plus Sophie had worked hard to earn that money. Her hand was *still* sore. And now twelve—well, eleven—people had vocabulary lists for free. That did not seem very fair to her.

But then a funny thing happened. Giving the money back got easy. Mostly because it made everyone so happy. And that made Sophie happy, too.

"Really?" Sydney said when Sophie gave back her dollar. "So you wrote my list for free? Wow. That's so nice. Thank you!"

"Thanks, Sophie. I can use the dollar for the book fair now!" Mia told her.

Dean was even happier. When Sophie gave back his five-dollar bill, he looked like he'd found an old friend.

"It's the first five dollars I ever got. Thank you, Sophie!" he said.

Sophie felt kind of cozy inside. Like she and Dean had shared a hug. But they had not. Thank goodness! Dean was so big she might get crushed.

By the time she'd given all the money back, Sophie almost didn't miss it. In fact, she almost wanted to give more of it out. . . .

A thought was hitting Sophie. Not hard and fast, like a snowball. But slow and gentle, like a bath.

It felt good to get money. But it felt good to give it, too.

And then another thought hit Sophie. This time like a snowball. Exactly!

Maybe she shouldn't be Sophie the Zillionaire. Maybe she should be Sophie the *Giver* instead!

But what about all the things she wanted to buy? She guessed she really did not need them.

And who knew? Even if Sophie made more

money than Mindy, Mindy's grandma could always give her more.

Sophie might never be richer than Mindy. But she could *give* more than her, for sure! What a great thing to be known for!

Suddenly, Sophie couldn't wait to get home. To get her bank and dump the money out. To change all her dollars into pennies. And to give it all to Hayley's class!

Or at least, a lot of it. Maybe she would keep a little. She could sure use some new rain boots. And some pink nail polish, too.

The day seemed to go on forever. Even art and gym and recess seemed slow. Finally, the bell rang and the bus took Sophie home.

She hugged Kate and said good-bye. Then Sophie ran home and up to her room. She bent down, reached under her bed, and pulled out . . .

Nothing.

Nothing?

Nothing!

Sophie reached back even further. She felt side to side. All around.

Finally, she crawled under the bed.

She saw lots of crumbs. And lots and lots of dust.

A-choo!

Oh. And her missing rain boot. So that's where it was.

But where was Sophie's horse bank?

She looked and looked and looked.

Sophie wiggled out from under her bed.

"Help! We've been robbed!" she yelled.

CHAPTER 10

Sophie ran to find her mom. She was in her own room, down the hall.

Sophie's mom looked up as she burst through the door. "Sophie! Hi! Have you seen Daddy's business cards?" she asked.

But Sophie did not have time for questions!

"Mom! We've been robbed!" she said.

Her mom shook her head. "Now, what would robbers do with Daddy's business cards?"

Sophie shook her own head very fast. "No, Mom. I'm not talking about that. I'm talking about *money*! I'm talking about robbers coming in and taking *that*!"

She waited for her mom to call the cops. But her mom did not reach for the phone. So Sophie picked it up.

"Do you call 911 for bank robberies?" Sophie asked.

"Hold on!" said her mom. She took the phone from Sophie and set it down. Then she sat on her bed and pulled Sophie beside her. "What makes you think there has been a bank robbery here?"

"Well . . . ," Sophie said. It was very simple. "My horse bank was under my bed this morning. Now it is not. I did not touch it. So it must have been robbed. Did you lock the door when you went out today?" she asked.

"I didn't go out. I've been home all day with Max," her mom said.

"Oh." Sophie bit her lip. *Hmm.* That made robbing her bank tricky. "Well, did anyone come over?" she asked.

Sophie's mom shrugged. "Just the cable guy, and Cole, Max's playdate."

"Aha!" Sophie held up her finger. "Then the robber is one of *them*!"

"But!" Sophie's mom held up her own finger. "Max and Cole played outside. And I was with the cable guy the whole time he was here."

"Oh," Sophie said. She bit her lip again.

Just then, something grabbed her foot! It came from under the bed.

"*Ahh!*" Sophie yelled.

The robber! He must have been hiding!

Sophie looked down. But there was no robber.

There was just Max.

"Come here, Maxie!" Sophie's mom said. She scooped him up, but he wriggled away.

Sophie's mom got up to follow the trail of graham cracker crumbs he left behind him. But first she turned to Sophie. "Honey, I'm sorry your bank is missing. But we were not robbed today. Trust me. You'll find it," she said.

Sophie sighed. That was easy for her to say.

☆ ☆ ☆

Sophie kept looking. But horse banks did not jump up and run off by themselves. She knew that for a fact. *Magic* horse banks, maybe. But Sophie's was not magic. She was pretty sure of that.

So who had taken it?

Sophie sat on her bed and tried to think.

Who knew where she hid her bank?

Who knew it was so full?

Who would want to take her money?

That was just when Hayley walked in.

Aha! Sophie thought.

"Where were you this morning? Between the hours of seven-thirty and eight?" she asked.

Hayley shrugged. "I don't know. Eating breakfast?" she said.

Sophie crossed her arms. "A likely story!"

"You were with me," Hayley said.

Oh . . . yeah.

"And after that?" asked Sophie.

"After that, I brushed my teeth. You were with

me then, too. Then we went to school. What's with all the questions?" Hayley asked.

Sophie jumped down, pulled up the bed skirt, and pointed. "I was robbed! My bank is gone!"

"Oh. That's too bad." Hayley shrugged again.

Sophie looked up at her. "That's too bad for *you*, you mean!" she said.

"How?" Hayley asked.

"Because I was going to give you that fifty dollars. For your penny drive," Sophie said.

"Really?" Hayley's eyes got big.

Sophie nodded. "Uh-huh. But now I can't be rich *or* give! It's just not fair!"

"Well, are you sure it's gone?" asked Hayley. She got down next to Sophie, beside the bed. Together, they peeked under the bed skirt again.

"Sure I'm sure. See? Nothing but my boot and crumbs and dust," Sophie said.

"Gross!" Hayley said. "You know, you shouldn't eat under your bed."

Sophie frowned. "I don't!" she told her.

"Then how did crumbs get there?" Hayley asked.

Sophie shrugged. She did not know.

Then, all of a sudden . . . she did!

Sophie jumped up. Fast!

"*Max!*" she yelled.

Sophie ran to Max's room. He had a graham cracker in one hand. It was making lots of crumbs. And he had Sophie's horse bank in his other hand! His cowboy doll was riding it.

"Max! That's *my* horse bank!" Sophie reached down and took it away.

Max started to howl. Of course. But Sophie did not care that much. She was used to it.

"What's going on?" their mom called from the hall.

Sophie covered her ears. "I just solved the Missing Horse Bank Mystery!" she yelled.

☆ ☆ ☆

Sophie learned two things that day.

One was that it was much better to keep things on her shelf than under her bed.

And the other was that she was good at solving mysteries. Very good, in fact.

So good that maybe that should be her name—Sophie the Snoop!

Hmm . . .

It was hard to pick!

"Sophie the Giver" was nice. And when Sophie gave Hayley the fifty dollars, her mom and Hayley made a very big deal about it.

"Mom, look what Sophie gave me for my penny drive!" Hayley said.

"Sophie! That is so generous! What a wonderful way to spend it!" her mom said.

Sophie and Hayley wanted to take fifty dollars to the bank to trade it for pennies. Right then. But their mom said it was fine to give the bill "as is." After all, fifty dollars was the same as five thousand pennies. And five thousand pennies would be very hard to carry. Plus, who knew?

That might be more pennies than the bank had, Sophie thought.

On the other hand, snooping was fun. And "Sophie the Snoop" would look so good on a business card.

Then Sophie thought about how her dad was missing his business cards now.

Oops. Maybe she should have asked for them first. As soon as he got home, Sophie would give them back to him.

But as soon as he got home, her dad gave *her* something instead.

"Surprise!" he said to Sophie and everyone else.

Then he passed out some other cards. They were big and shiny and colorful.

Sophie's mom crossed her arms. "Are these what I think they are?" she asked.

Sophie's dad grinned. "If you think they're scratch-off lottery tickets, then yes!" he said.

Sophie's mom rolled her eyes.

But Sophie did not. What she did was start scratching—very hard!

She did not care about being rich anymore. But still, it wouldn't be bad. Then she could give away more money. And buy a real detective hat!

All she had to do was match three numbers. How easy was that?

She scratched off two **100**s!

Then two **1,000**s!

Then a **2**.

And a **5**.

And a **20**.

And another **100**?

Yes!

No.

It was just a **10**.

Sophie looked at her lottery card again. And again. But there were no threes of anything.

Too bad. Her mom was right about the lottery. It wasn't a very good way to make money after all, she guessed.

Then, suddenly, her mom started jumping. She hugged Sophie's dad and waved her card.

"I won fifty dollars!" she cried.

No way! Sophie thought.

"Congratulations!" Sophie's dad said. "What are you going to buy?"

Sophie's mom grinned and shook her head. "Nothing! I'm going to give it to Hayley's penny drive—just like Sophie," she said.

Sophie felt tingly from her bangs to her toes. More people were giving. All thanks to her!

Now—back to *snooping* . . .

If she could just find another mystery to solve!

Sophie's new name is right around the corner. Could this one be a perfect fit?

Take a peek at Sophie's next adventure....

What a day! Sophie thought.

Because today was the day she was *something.* And that something was Sophie the *Snoop.*

Yes! That was who she was from now on.

More than anything, Sophie wanted to be extra-special. To be extra-great at . . . *something.* She had tried to be great at *everything* at first. But that was hard. So then she had tried to be great at one thing. Like being a hero. Or being honest. Or being rich. But that was hard, too.

Then, suddenly, it came to her in a great big *whoosh.* Sophie was great at solving mysteries. She was a natural snoop!

First she solved the Missing Horse Bank Mystery, just like that. (The thief had been her little brother, Max.)

Then she solved the Mystery of the Missing Business Cards. (Of course, that wasn't really a mystery. *Sophie* had taken her dad's cards. But he never would have found them without her. That was a fact.)

Now Sophie the Snoop could not wait to solve her next case—whatever it was!

So she was very ready when her mom called out, "It's almost time to go to school. Hey! Who left the toilet seat up?"

Sophie tiptoed to the downstairs bathroom—the scene of the crime. (She knew that snoops tiptoed, so she had to. But she did it very fast.)

"This is a case for Sophie the Snoop, Mom!" she cried.

Sophie looked around the bathroom and found a clue almost right away. It was the mug she had painted for her dad's birthday. She picked it up off the sink.

"Aha!" she said.

Sophie flashed her mom a smile and headed for the kitchen. Her dad was waiting by the toaster for something to pop up. Sophie tiptoed up behind him and shouted, "Gotcha!"

Her dad turned, surprised, and saw the mug. He sighed and held up his hands. "Sure enough. That's my mug. Guilty as charged," he told her.

Sophie smiled. She crossed her arms. "No case is too tough for Sophie the Snoop!" she declared.